Whisked Away

Written by Timothy Knapman

Illustrated by Alfredo Belli

Collins

1 Baker Jake

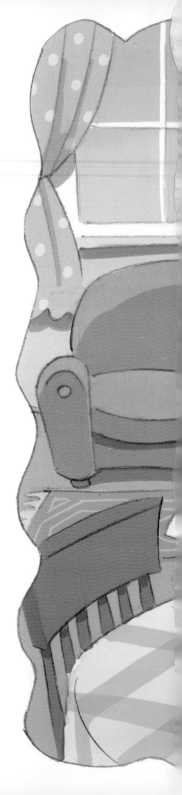

Baker Jake loved baking from
the moment he first tasted
his granny's sponge cake.
It was only a mouthful, but
the sweetness and softness
of the cake seemed to fill
his whole body with a tingly,
zingly feeling of happiness.

When Jake's granny told
him she had baked the
cake herself, Jake begged
to know how.

She listed the ingredients –
the butter, the eggs, the sugar,
the flour – but Jake still
couldn't understand how
she had turned them into
something so wonderful.

So Jake's granny said,
"I'll show you."

Jake didn't take his eyes off his granny as she softened the butter and cracked the eggs, sprinkled the sugar and added the flour.

"Now," she said, "I'm going to let you into the greatest secret of cake baking, but you must promise never to tell another living soul."

"I promise," said Jake, feeling very big all of a sudden.

"There's a special ingredient in all really good cakes," his granny explained, "and that special ingredient is love."

Sponge cake
butter
eggs
sugar
flour
SPECIAL INGREDIENT
(SHHH!)

"How do you get love into a cake?" asked Jake.

"You whisk it in," said his granny, and she rummaged in a drawer and pulled out a strange object. It had a wooden handle from which long loops of metal stretched and twisted. "This is my special whisk," said Jake's granny. It didn't look special, it looked old: the handle was loose and some of the metal loops were tangled and bent. Jake thought it might break at any moment but, as he watched his granny use it to mix up the ingredients, he saw how well it did the job.

"Now it's your turn," said his granny, handing Jake the bowl and the whisk. "Remember to shut your eyes and think good, loving thoughts: that way, you will whisk love into the cake."

Jake shut his eyes and remembered how good it felt to cuddle his cat. He whisked until the ingredients in the bowl had mixed into a silky smooth batter that was filled with love.

When the new cake was baked and cooled and filled with jam and cream and dusted with sugar, Jake took a bite. It tasted even better than the first one.

Jake's granny saw how much he'd enjoyed baking and so she gave him her whisk. "Remember," she said, "the secret ingredient."

When he was older, Jake went to baking school.
He learnt how to make every kind of cake,
from the smallest cupcake to the tallest toffee coffee
brownie stack with chopped nuts on top. He always
used his granny's whisk because it was the only
way he knew how to mix the secret ingredient into
his cakes.

At last, Jake opened his very own cake shop.
Word soon spread about his wonderful cakes,
and people came from miles around to buy them.
They asked Jake what he put in his cakes that made
them taste so special.

"I use only fresh, natural ingredients," Jake told them.

"Is that all?" they asked.

10

Jake remembered his promise to his granny and just smiled.

It wasn't long before food magazines and websites and television programmes declared that Jake baked "The Very Best Cakes in the World!"

2 Auntie Maureen

"I demand a competition!"
roared Maureen Buttercream from behind
her huge desk at the vast headquarters of
her gigantic company "Auntie Maureen's
Cakes-U-Like". Maureen's company
sold millions of cakes every year, so she
was very angry when she heard that
Baker Jake's cakes had been named
"The Very Best Cakes in the World".

"What kind of competition?"
asked her assistant, Martin Rissole.

"A television cake-baking competition,
of course!" snapped Maureen rudely.
"It will be the greatest there
has ever been – for this one will
feature … me! The mightiest
baker the world has ever known!
Then everyone watching will see
me triumph over this wretched little
Jake person and realise how rotten
his awful cakes are."

"Of course," said Martin Rissole, who had learnt the hard way that you never argued with Maureen. "You do know that he makes his cakes himself from only fresh, natural ingredients, don't you?"

"So what?" sneered Maureen.

"Well, we make ours in huge greasy machines," said Martin Rissole. "Then we pump them full of chemicals so they'll last for months."

"Well, isn't that nice of us?" said Maureen.

"I just think – " said Martin Rissole slowly, and then he speeded up so he could say everything he wanted before Maureen had a chance to throw the desk at him, "that his cakes might be … more scrummy than ours and you'll lose the competition in front of millions of people and no one will ever eat our cakes again and we'll be ruined."

Maureen's face went a very angry shade of bright red, but before she could open her mouth, Martin gave her a cardboard box. Inside, was a small fruit cake.

"It's from Baker Jake's shop," said Martin. "I thought you should try it."

Maureen reached into the box and pulled a small piece off the cake. She sniffed it, then put it in her mouth, chewing and tasting it very carefully.

"Bleurgh!" Maureen spat. "This cake *isn't* delicious! Oh no. It's *far* worse than that! This cake is *heavenly*! It is pure happiness in the form of a cake." Her eyes narrowed suspiciously.

"He makes his cakes out of 'fresh, natural ingredients'
you say? No, no. There's something else in here:
a *secret* ingredient that he isn't telling anyone about.
If we find out what that is, we can beat him! We can
cream him! We can knock his filling out!" And she
laughed an evil laugh.

3 The secret

Maureen spent the next
week in her cake laboratory.
She did everything she
could to find out what
Jake's secret ingredient was.
She put the fruit cake under
a microscope, she chopped
it up with lasers, and she
even fed it into a computer
– though the computer
did stop working
shortly afterwards.

At the end of the week,
she still had no idea.

"Spy on this Baker Jake,"
she commanded
Martin Rissole. "Find out
his secret, but hurry –
the baking competition
is tomorrow!"

Baker Jake felt very nervous about taking part in a television competition with the famous Maureen Buttercream, who was rich and successful and bound to win. He decided to cheer himself up by doing some baking. He got out his granny's whisk, closed his eyes and thought good, loving thoughts as he mixed the ingredients. When it had become a perfect batter, Jake opened his eyes – and saw that someone was looking at him! A man in a pretend beard sitting up in a tree was watching him through binoculars! But why?

"Excuse me!" Jake called out to him.

"Oh. What? No!" said the man, and he fell out of the tree, dropping both his binoculars and his pretend beard. He picked them both up and tried to stick his binoculars onto his chin. "Oops, wrong one!" he said, sticking his pretend beard back onto his chin instead as he ran off.

The next morning, Jake arrived at the television studio where the competition was taking place.

Ingrid Blizzard, a jolly woman who was going to present the programme, welcomed him. "We've set up a kitchen for you and one for Auntie Maureen. Do you have everything you need?"

All Jake needed was his granny's whisk and that was safe in the little bag in his hand.

Jake's granny had come along to wish him luck. When he took out the whisk and put it on a worktop, she said, "You're not still using that old thing!"

"How else could I mix in the special ingredient?" Jake replied.

Before his granny could answer, Maureen arrived. The man with her looked familiar but Jake couldn't think why, and just like that, Ingrid said, "It's time to get started."

4 The competition

The audience clapped as Ingrid came out to say hello to them. "Welcome," she went on, "to this once-in-a-lifetime competition to decide who really does bake the very best cakes in the world."

"The final decision will be made by our judges, who are both famous food experts. We have Hugo Dare –" Ingrid pointed to a brave-looking man. "In his long career, Hugo has travelled the world, eating everything you can eat, and quite a lot that you shouldn't."

"Yes, keep away from tarantula pancakes!" said Hugo.

"And Elena Wimple, whose taste buds are so powerful she can tell you the flavour of an ice cream from over a mile away just by sticking her tongue out."

"Mint choc chip," said Elena, and she put her tongue back in.

"So now –" said Ingrid. "No more waiting –
let's get baking!"

Maureen was very fast.
Her hands shot out
to gather ingredients
so quickly, it was
like watching
a robot at work.

Jake, meanwhile, wasn't doing anything.

"You don't have time to think about things,"
Ingrid reminded him.

Jake wasn't thinking, however: he was frozen
with dread. His granny's whisk had disappeared!
Where could it have gone? And more importantly,
how was he going to mix the special ingredient into
his cake? Then he had a shocking thought: someone
must have stolen it!

Baker Jake looked over at Maureen. She was going even faster now. She had already buttered and lined her cake tin and was pouring in the batter! Any minute now, she'd be mixing her filling! She caught his eye and grinned wickedly at him. She knew she was going to win!

At that moment, Jake realised where he'd seen Maureen's friend before. He was the man in the tree who'd been spying on him!

"He wanted to know how I make my cakes," thought Jake. "He must have stolen the whisk so that Maureen would win!"

There was no time to do anything about it now. If he was going to bake, he had to start right away.

Jake collected the ingredients in a bowl, but how was he going to mix them? The only thing he could find in the drawers was a fork. How could he mix love into his cake with an ordinary fork? Jake closed his eyes and thought of every good and lovely thing. It all felt very odd, but he had no choice. He slipped the cake into the oven and spent all the cooking time hoping things would somehow work out.

Jake was just piping the last line of icing on his cake, when Ingrid cried, "Time's up!"

5 The Very Best Cakes in the World!

Jake had made a small chocolate
cake with creamy fudge filling.
Maureen, meanwhile, had made
a stunning five-layer rainbow fairy tale
castle cake that almost touched the ceiling:
it looked amazing! There was no way she
could lose.

"Wow!" said Hugo, as he walked around
Maureen's cake.

"There's lots of flavour," said Elena,
as she tasted it. "Mmm ... but
something's missing."

When the judges saw Jake's cake,
they looked at one another disappointedly.
"I was hoping for a bit more imagination,"
said Hugo. "Let's see how it tastes."

They each took a piece. They tasted it
carefully, wrinkled their noses and looked
at each other. They took another piece ...

Then they took another piece, and another and another.

"Hang on!" said Ingrid. "What do you think?"

Hugo made a noise through a mouthful of cake.

"It's … awful?" asked Ingrid, trying to work out what he'd said.

Instead of answering at once, Hugo just took another slice and crammed it into his mouth and made another noise.

"You're saying it's – " said Ingrid, trying to work it out "– scrumptious?"

Hugo and Elena nodded their heads excitedly and reached for more cake.

"So Jake's the winner?" asked Ingrid.

"Of course he is!" said the judges, spraying Ingrid with half-chewed crumbs because they just couldn't stop eating Jake's cake.

The audience erupted in cheers.

Maureen waited till she was alone with Martin before she started shouting at him. "This is all your fault! You were supposed to find out what his secret is!"

Before Martin could reply, Jake caught up with them.

"I just wanted to say thank you for asking me to bake with you. It was a great honour," said Jake, shaking Maureen's hand, "and may I have my whisk back, please?"

"You stole his whisk?" Maureen snapped at Martin. "*That's* his secret? Why didn't you give it to me?"

"I didn't take your whisk, Jake," said Martin. "It's true I spied on you, and I'm sorry about that, but I couldn't work out what your secret was. Except that I saw you close your eyes as you whisked."

"Well, if *you* didn't take my whisk, who did?" asked Jake.

"It was me," said a voice. Everyone whirled round to see … Jake's granny standing there with a shopping bag. "The moment I saw you still had it, I knew I had to get you a new one immediately."

"A new one?" said Jake. "But it's the only way to mix in the special ingredient!"

"Are you sure?" asked Jake's granny. "Congratulations on winning, by the way."

Jake realised: he *had* won without using the old whisk.

"The whisk isn't important," said his granny. "The special ingredient is."

"Will someone please tell me what this secret ingredient is?" asked Maureen desperately.

Jake had promised his granny that he would never tell another living soul, but his granny took pity on Maureen and said, "It's love."

"*That's* why you close your eyes when you whisk," said Martin.

"But I bake all *my* cakes with love too," said Maureen.

"You *used to*, Auntie," Martin replied. "When you were baking just for me, your nephew. Then you got more and more successful and busier and you didn't have time to put love into your cakes – or into your life."

At first, Maureen didn't believe him. Then she thought for a moment and nodded. "You're right. I didn't even realise what was happening. I just got so busy baking more and more cakes, and wanting to be the very best, that I lost sight of why I was baking them in the first place. The busier I got, the more bad-tempered I became. Please forgive me."

"Of course I do," said Martin, and he and Maureen hugged.

"That's better," said Jake's granny, and she reached into her bag. "Now is anyone else feeling hungry after all this excitement? Only I've brought this cake with me and I think it's high time we all had a slice."

The recipe for a really good story

Stories are like cakes: they are made up of ingredients that must be put together in just the right way.

① Take one hero

② Add a villain

③ Mix them together

4) Sprinkle in some spying

5) and surprises (Did YOU guess that it was Jake's granny who had taken his whisk?) and top with a really good ending.

6) Most important of all – NEVER FORGET THE SECRET INGREDIENT! Just like cakes, stories are to be enjoyed, so always make them with love – and just a dash of mischief.

Ideas for reading

Written by Christine Whitney
Primary Literacy Consultant

Reading objectives:
- discuss the sequence of events in books
- make inferences on the basis of what is being said and done
- answer and ask questions
- predict what might happen on the basis of what has been read so far

Spoken language objectives:
- ask relevant questions to extend their understanding and knowledge
- use spoken language to develop understanding through speculating, hypothesising, imagining and exploring ideas
- participate in discussions, role play and improvisations

Curriculum links: Design and technology – use the principles of a healthy and varied diet to prepare dishes and understand where food comes from

Word count: 2538

Interest words: whisk, chemicals, laboratory

Resources: exercise book and pencils; handheld balloon whisk – like the one used in the book

Build a context for reading

- Show children a whisk similar to the type used in the book. Ask them to name the object and to discuss what it might be used for. Have they used a whisk before?

- Read the title and look at the image on the front cover. Ask children to explain what the illustration tells the reader about the main character. How do they know this?

- Read the blurb together. Look at the illustration on the back cover and discuss what has changed from the cover illustration. Ask children to predict what might happen to the baker in the story.

- Discuss the meaning of the word *laboratory*. How might this word fit into the story?